Mary Black

TRAVELS IN TIME

VENETIAN CRETE

Illustration: Roussetos Panagiotakis

Mary Black was born in Herakleion, the largest city of Crete. Her first impressions and literary influences came from the Greek fairy tales she listened to. Captain Nemo, the Young Prince, and Hansel and Gretel became her companions and formed the material from which she drew to make stories for children. She studied music and political science. For a number of years, she wrote opinion articles for local newspapers of Herakleion. She started her travels from the places she describes in her stories. Her first four books are in the series The Time-machine Diaries, titled Travels in Time: Minoan Crete, Venetian Crete, The Battle of Crete, and Alexander the Great in Pergamum. She has written many other books for children: Magic Bible, Fairy tales, Travel in the Sun, The four seasons and the abduction of Persephone. Her books have awarded from Reader's favorite and International Art Society.

Travels in time Venetian Crete
by Mary Black
Copyright © Mary Mavrogiannaki, 2015
www.mbbooks.gr
Translated by
Demetrios P. Dallas
Artwork by
Roussetos Panagiotakis
Poem by
Xrysoula Stefanaki
Herakleion 2015

Candia looks like mist on the horizon.
Above her a cloud foretells a storm:
a storm of centuries.

INTRODUCTION

Four children from Crete – Alex, Irene, Kostantis and Nikolas – followed an old map to Koules, the Venetian castle of Heraklio in Crete. It was here they discovered the time machine.

Then, quite by mistake, Kostantis set the machine running and transported them all to Minoan Crete. Ariadne came too – an archaeologist who wanted to steal the machine for herself.

The time travellers, aided by the court official Zakros and his nephew Radamanthys, managed to seek help from King Minos. In his palace in Knossos, they tried to set the machine to return them home. But at that moment a great earthquake shook the timer, and the four friends, caught in a time-eddy, found themselves once again in a faraway place, at the beginning of another adventure.

CHAPTER 1

Irene was the first to come-to after the time-jump.
She realized she was still holding Radamanthys'
present, and unfolded the wrapping with a look of
wonder. It looked like the inscribed disc of
Phaestos.

She tried to read the Minoan script but couldn't.
Nor could she speak the Minoan language as she
had just hours before. She glanced around her.
Nothing looked as it should.

"Wake up!" she called to her friends.

Alex rose, blinking wearily, then gave a fearful
look at their surroundings – a few scant buildings
and some hedgerow on the edge of an anonymous
town.

"Do you know where we are?"

"I've no idea."

Nikolas and Kostantis woke too.

"Where are we now?"

"We don't know," Alex said.

Nikolas turned to Kostantis. "You tell us! You programmed the date on the time-machine!"

"I'm sure I set the temporal parameters correctly," Kostantis said, rubbing his eyes. "I think the earthquake must have destabilized the time-meter."

"Was it the earthquake, or you when you fell on it?"

As usual, the two boys started arguing.

"Stop!" Irene shouted. "We need to keep our heads. Does anyone have any idea where we are?"

"I do," said a familiar voice.

All of them turned at once. They saw Ariadne standing behind them, still in her Minoan clothing.

"Have you followed us again?" Irene said.

"I've missed you," she smiled.

"But how did you manage to travel?" Kostantis said. "You weren't with us when the machine started up."

"When I came into the room you were gone, but the time-gate was still open. I jumped in, and pronto," she said, "here I am."

Irene looked ready to scream at her.

"Come on," Nikolas shouted. "This isn't the time to settle our differences with Ariadne. We should find a good place to hide and fix the time machine."

They started off without knowing where they were going, nor what dangers and adventures this strange place had in store. They'd walked in silence for a while, lost in thought, when they heard the sound of horses galloping towards them.

"Look out!" Alex said. They ran for cover behind some bushes, holding their breaths.

Three riders clad in chainmail stopped just in front of their hiding place. They clambered down, took off their helmets and led their horses to a babbling spring a few yards away. The young soldiers waited patiently while the animals drank.

As they talked, the children realized again that they could understand the language, just as they could in Minoan Crete.

"Morosini is preparing a feast for our saint's day tomorrow," the tallest said.

"Yes, I heard, Vincenzo," the second answered. "A two-day ceasefire has been called as well. We may stand down for a few hours. But I must admit those Cretans are brave soldiers."

"We've all seen it, Angelo," Vincenzo said. "They're a proud people. I admire them. What do you say, Fabio?"

"They fight like lions upon the battlements," Fabio said. "I haven't been here long, but I believe their courage and valour."

"Tell me, Fabio, why you, a nobleman's son, left Venice to come here?"

"I needed action. I was tired of the endless feasting at Doge Contarinis' palazzo. But now we must go, I think. I'm expected at the duke's palace."

The three mounted their horses and rode away. The children and the archaeologist at last emerged from the bushes.

"Who were they? What language was that?" Nikolas said.

Ariadne looked thoughtfully at him. "Those were Venetian soldiers," she said. "We're close to Heraklion. These are the times of Venetian rule. The language we're going to hear is Italo-Cretan, a Greek dialect with a lot of Venetian and Italian words and phrases, mixed with the vocabulary and expressions of the Cretan idiom."

"Are you sure we're in Venetian Crete?" Kostantis said.

"Certain! Didn't you notice the coat of arms on their chainmail and their horses' caparison? It's the winged lion of Venice, the symbol of the Serenissima Republic. How convenient that we've ended up near our homes, even though, as usual, we're in the wrong era." The archaeologist couldn't hide a note of satisfaction in her voice.

"And how do you know we're near Heraklio and not in a different part of Crete?" Nikolas said.

"The soldiers, as you must have noticed, said that Morosini is holding a religious feast. Duke Francesco Morosini had his base at Candia. That was the name of Heraklio in the years of Venetian rule."

"Hey," Alex said. "Isn't that the same Morosini who's going to surrender Candia to Köprülü?"

"I suppose so," Kostantis said. "We must be at Candia during the long siege. But didn't it last for twenty-two years until 1669, when the city was surrendered to the Turks?"

"Your knowledge comes as a pleasant surprise," Ariadne smiled.

"We aren't that ignorant, even if we aren't archaeologists. I suppose we know a thing or two," Kostantis said.

Nikolas was listening impatiently, and finally jumped in: "Why don't we put off the history lecture for now and try to make a plan?"

"We should get into the city," Ariadne said. "At least to find out what year it is."

"How are we going to do it in these clothes?" Irene smiled. "People didn't wear jeans and hoodies during the Renaissance."

Ariadne sighed. "I'll find you some clothing. After all, my outfit is closer to that of the era."

"But you're wearing Minoan clothes."

"I may draw a little attention, but they'll probably think it's a new fashion I brought from the West."

"How are you going to find us clothes?" Kostantis said.

"I'll think of something. You'd better stay in hiding until I return."

"Are you going to sell that necklace you're wearing?" Irene said.

"Never!" Ariadne touched the golden bee-engraved pendant hanging from her neck. "This is a gift from King Minos, and I'm never, ever going to part with it."

Irene unzipped her satchel and pulled out Radamanthys' gift. She stepped close to Ariadne saying, "Take this. Buy whatever we need."

Ariadne opened the package and stared at its contents in wonder. It was the inscribed disc of Phaestos. "Do you know what this is?" she said.

"Yes." Irene lowered her eyes.

"Do you understand what's written on it?"

"Yes."

"Then tell me!"

"It's a prayer to the Mother-Goddess of the Minoans."

"Are you sure? Have you read it?"

"I didn't have time. When we arrived here, I couldn't read the Minoan any more. Radamanthys told me it's an invocation to the Mother-Goddess."

"That's amazing!" Ariadne gasped. "Do you understand what a rare find this is?"

"To me it only has sentimental value," Irene said.

"We can't sell it. This is our heritage. As General Makriyannis said, during the War of Independence, 'Those ancient stones are what we fought for'. I'll think of something else, I'm sure, to buy us the things we need." Ariadne turned quickly, and made for the city.

"I don't trust her," Irene puffed as she watched her walk. "She might just leave us here, given the chance."

"As long as we have the machine, we can't shake her off," Alex said, putting a hand on her shoulder.

"Let's hope you're right. We all remember the trouble she caused with King Minos. We almost lost our lives. It's this terrible wish she has to change the course of history and—"

"Look at those trees," Kostantis shouted. "They're full of fruit, and I'm starving."

It was gone noon, and they all realized they were getting hungry.

"Let's eat," Alex said. "Or my rumbling stomach will blow our cover."

The four friends made their way in an arbour of apple-, orange- and lemon-trees heavy with fruit. They munched on the produce of Cretan soil, which tasted so much like home. Their hunger abated for the moment.

"We must go back," Nikolas said, biting deeply into the flesh of an orange. "Ariadne may already be waiting for us."

The four returned to their meeting-point, but there was no sign of Ariadne. They kept watch, expecting her to appear, and slowly grew more afraid and dejected. Then they heard voices and ran to hide again. They saw men with laden donkeys heading for the building across from the fountain.

"What is that place?" Kostantis asked.

"It looks like a warehouse," Alex whispered.

"They're granaries," Ariadne said as she appeared in front of them, holding a large package. "What you know as the Lions Square is called here Cereals Square, or *Piazza delle Biade*."

She was wearing a long, sky-blue dress with gold-embroidered front. Her hair was covered in a silk headscarf.

"You made it back," Irene said.

"I did. Now, all of you change. We're too exposed out here." And with these words she gave each of them a change of clothes.

They stepped behind a row of trees, while Irene chose some bushes as a changing-room. There were breeches, white shirts, sashes and laced boots for the boys. Alex and Kostantis put on short white headscarves, while Nikolas was given a small red *fez*. Irene's lot was a long purple skirt, a white shirt, and a velvet jerkin with beautiful needlework. On her head she placed an embroidered purple headscarf.

"You look terrific," Ariadne cried out when she saw them emerging from the trees. "As you can see, the clothes of Cretans in this time weren't much different from our traditional clothing."

"Your dress is different," Irene noted.

"Such gold-embroidered dresses are worn by the Venetian or Cretan noble maidens, who followed the European fashions," she smiled. "You're wearing the more traditional garb."

"How did you find such beautiful and expensive clothing?" Irene asked.

Ariadne was suddenly angry. "Look, what does it matter? I took care of all of us."

Irene noticed she wasn't wearing her golden-bee pendant any more. She was saddened by that but said nothing, imagining how painful it must have been for Ariadne to sell a piece of jewellery given to her by King Minos.

But Nikolas couldn't contain himself. "Why did you give me a Turkish *fez*? I'm not going to wear it, ever!"

"You're wrong, Nikolas," she said. "What you're wearing isn't even remotely related to the *fez*. Now that we're going into town, you'll see that locals are wearing it too."

"She's right," Kostantis said. "During the years of Venetian rule, Cretans would wear either a short headscarf or a little *fez*. I read somewhere they also took to wearing breeches after the Algerian pirates."

"Correct," Ariadne said with a smile. "The traditional Cretan clothing for men is very much like that of the Algerian Zouaves."

Nikolas looked befuddled. "Who are they?"

"The Zouaves, or Zouaoua, were an Algerian tribe that lived on the Jurjura Range. They were Berbers and provided soldiers for Algiers and Tunis."

"Never mind all this," Kostantis said. "Do you know now where we are?"

She straightened his headscarf "This is the Idomeneus Fountain, behind our own Chandakos Street. If we walk uphill from here, we'll get to the Lions Square."

"But I'm hungry now," Kostantis said.

"We're all hungry. We'll have to find a tavern or inn, where we can eat and find out more about the year. When it gets dark, we'll have to find a hotel or inn, pay for some rooms, and set up the time-machine at our leisure. Are we agreed?"

They were nodding as a middle-aged man and a girl stopped by the fountain to draw water.

"Good afternoon to you, noble maidens and masters," the man said.

"Good afternoon to you too, good sir," Ariadne said, observing him with interest.

He was wearing frayed breeches, black shirt and headscarf, and well-worn laced boots. The girl was dressed in a white shirt, long green skirt, crimson jerkin, apron, and knitted jacket with threadbare sleeves.

"Are you new in town?" he said. "I haven't seen you before."

"Yes. We've just arrived."

"On that ship I saw coming in today from Venice, no doubt, with munitions and supplies?"

Ariadne looked at the others. "Yes, that's the one."

"And where are you staying, if I may ask?" he said, looking carefully at their clothes.

"Nowhere yet. Do you know of somewhere we might rest?"

"You've met the right man," he beamed. "I own an inn just around the corner. Not much in the way of luxury, but it's clean – and my daughter here's an excellent cook."

"I think it'll suit us," Ariadne said.

"I'll bring a table to the courtyard, so that you can enjoy the view of the harbour as you eat. The weather feels more like July than April. And we must provide every comfort for nobility like yourselves."

"Where's your inn?" Kostantis said.

"Here, close to St Peter's – blessed be his Grace!" He made the sign of the cross.

Irene proffered her hand. "My name is Irene. This is Kostantis, Nikolas and Alex."

"My name is Ariadne," offered the archaeologist.

"I'm Manousos," the man said, warmly shaking Irene's hand. Glancing at the maiden with the earthenware jug he added, "My daughter's name is Arete. Let's go! You look tired. You must have journeyed long."

"We've been travelling for ages!" Alex said with a laugh.

CHAPTER 2

The inn was an old two-storey building with a sea view, and their innkeeper set a table for them under a blooming lemon tree in the courtyard. The soft tang of the sea and the aroma of flowers helped them feel better about the place and the times, and they forgot their predicament for a while.

"Radamanthys' house must have been somewhere around here," Irene noted sadly.

"That's my impression too," Alex said. "Same view, same smells."

"Is he well now? Could he have survived the earthquake?" Irene wondered, looking out towards the sea.

"Get a grip on yourself," Nikolas snapped. "Even if he survived, he's been dead for a few thousand years."

"You're right, but we saw him for the last time just a few hours ago," she sighed.

"I guess it's the way we move through time," Ariadne said, "but you've lost your bearings."

"We must think about what we're going to do from now on," Kostantis cut in.

Nikolas sat quietly, with a look of dark premonition. Alex thought of his mother. She must be full of anxiety. Would he ever see her again? Tears welled in his eyes.

Ariadne was looking at the castle in awe. She remembered the words of Nikos Kazantzakis: "Capetan-Michalis' eyes were riveted to the Great Koules, a wide, brawny tower on the right as you enter the harbour, with the winged lion of Venice set in marble upon his chest."

She still found it hard to believe she had the ability to move in time, and to live in the history she'd been studying for so long. Her only desire was to wrest the machine from the youngsters and time-travel alone. And also – why shouldn't she? – to change events: to put things in place, to stop injustice and pain for all the suffering people in history – but predominantly for Cretans, who fought, generation upon generation, for their soil, their home, their liberty and their faith.

Manousos' voice broke off their ruminations. "I've brought you fresh bread, olives and cheese. There's a little wine in the pitcher. Our *malvasia* is renowned the world over. Merchants from come from hundreds of miles to buy it. My daughter is preparing meat casserole. Arete, my child," he called, "please take a jug to fill with fresh water."

The girl stepped from the inn to the courtyard with a jug on her right shoulder. She was a beautiful maiden of sixteen, shorter than average, wheat-complexioned, with large honey-coloured eyes and brown hair in braids that reached her back. Manousos turned to look at her. He was tall and wide, with close-cropped dark hair and brown skin.

Alex stood. "Please allow me to help you with the water," he told her. "That jug must be heavy for you when it's full."

The girl blushed a little, and answered him with downcast eyes. "Thank you, I don't need help, I'm used to it. Since my mother died, I'm doing all kinds of housework."

"Let this noble young man help you, if he wants to," her father said.

"If father allows it, follow me."

Manousos looked at his daughter with pride. His secret hope was somehow to arrange for her to leave the island alive, as the clouds of war were ever darkening over Candia.

Arete and Alex walked up the narrow street and turned into a thoroughfare.

"Where are we?"

"We're in the *Ruga Maistra*," Arete said. "We'll get water from the Morosini fountain, and you'll have a chance to admire the city.

To their right and left were two- or three-storey houses, stores and public buildings. Alex looked around him, feeling lost, even though he knew this was 25th August Street just a few centuries before his own time. There were more pedestrians now. Many of them men, some dressed in the traditional Cretan breeches, some in Venetian clothing. Others rode horses in chainmail. The few women in the street wore traditional Cretan or Venetian dresses down to their feet.

"Is this your first time in Candia?"

"Yes, in this era," Alex said.

She looked at him quizzically.

"Ignore me," he stuttered, his face flushed, as he realized he'd said more than he should.

On their way to the fountain they met a young maiden of the nobility escorted by two soldiers and a chaperone. Hers was a rare beauty, Alex thought. She was walking tall – like a doe; her skin was snow-white, and her long fair hair cascaded over her shoulders. Her eyes were the colour of the sea. She wore a long red dress with embroidered bust and a cape done in gold thread about her shoulders.

"Who is she?" he said.

"She's Bianca, Morosini's niece."

"Beautiful!"

"Yes, very," Arete said, looking at Bianca with a tender smile.

They continued to the *Loggia*, where Arete showed him the great edifice.

"This is the headquarters of Duke Francesco Morosini. All the nobles who govern our island meet here to discuss profound ideas. They talk for many hours sometimes. But things are getting more and more difficult," she told him.

"What do you mean?"

"I mean the siege," she said, puzzled again.

"Ah, of course. The Turks outside the city walls."

It's our worst fear, Alex thought. These are indeed the times of the long siege. But which year was it? He had to learn – that was essential – but how? He couldn't ask Arete, not now.

As she filled her water jug from the marble mouth of a lion's head in the fountain, he looked around him. He could see St Mark's bell tower and clock. Before it the saint's fiery standard fluttered in the wind.

"Do you want us to go inside and light a candle to the saint's grace?" Arete said, trying to deflect his embarrassment, which was incomprehensible to her. "It's the saint's day tomorrow, and we'll have a feast."

"So tomorrow must be the 25th of April," he mused. And then let it slip:

"But of which year?"

"Tomorrow is the 25th of April, in the year of our Saviour 1665," she said, bewildered. "Are you sure you're alright?"

"I'm just a little tired. We'd better go back."

She knew something strange was going on, but asked nothing that might make him uneasy. She had taken much pleasure in the strange boy's company.

On the way back, Alex silently took the jug from her shoulder and lifted it to his.
"You're late!" Ariadne said when she saw them. "Where have you been?"

"We walked to the Morosini fountain to get water," Alex sighed, heavy with anxiety about the siege.

Arete took the jug from his hands and filled all their cups with water. Then she fetched the cooking pot and served them their dinner in earthenware dishes.

Her father took her aside. "Did that noble lad tell you something?" he asked her.

"No, father. He just seems to be a bit confused."

"I don't blame him. He's just arrived in a city under siege. The Turkish cannonade won't stop. We've learned to live this way, but they have not. This noble maiden, Irene, may be your chance to leave the island. I might ask her to take you with her when she returns to Venice. Then you can travel to your mother's brother in Genoa – he'll certainly welcome you there. You're in danger here, child. How much longer can we go on fighting?"

"We're all in danger, father, not just me. I'm not going anywhere! We've lasted for so many years now. I'm sure sometime will be able to kick them out – Turks and Venetians too – and we'll breathe freely at last. And then we can travel together to Genoa, and I can study music, like mother."

Her father's eyes glistened. "Your mother was a great woman."

"She was a brave Cretan woman! She did her duty. I'll do the same if I need to," the girl said.

"She came from a noble line, your mother. Yet she loved me, and I was her inferior. So her family disowned her. And what did I give her? Poverty, until she died fighting the Turks…"

"But she was happy. She loved you so much!"

"Yes, and I adored her too. As long as I breathe, I'll remember her with love. She was a real noblewoman. Her family came from Byzantium. She was the descendant of the line of the twelve princes. It is for her sake I want you to have a better life, my child," the man said, his eyes full of tears.

"Don't be sad, father. We'll save our beloved Candia, you'll see."

Meanwhile, the five-time travellers were hungrily munching the dinner Arete had prepared for them.

As they were finishing, Alex whispered, "I have something unpleasant to tell you."

"What's going on?" Irene said.

"I've learned the date. Today is the 24th of April in the year 1665."

Kostantis looked up sharply. "We must leave as soon as we can."

"The Turks took Candia in 1669," Ariadne said. "There's no reason to be upset. We could even prevent them!"

"Don't even think about it!" Irene hissed. "We can't turn history upside-down. It's wrong for us to intervene, and you know it."

"But we could save Candia from the Turks," the archaeologist persisted. "What's wrong with that?"

"If we change history, we may cause something worse to happen."

"Alright, alright. When we finish eating, we'll take a walk through the city. When we return to the inn, we'll set the machine up and leave."

"I say we leave now," Nikolas said, looking dubiously at Ariadne.

"A stroll will do us good," she said. "I couldn't stand the thought that we left Candia's most glorious era without seeing those beautiful Venetian buildings."

"These people were conquerors," Kostantis said. "Just like the Arabs and Turks."

"I agree, but they turned Candia into a great commercial and cultural hub. They called the city 'little Venice'. They built the walls, the castle, the *Loggia*, St Mark's, the dockyards, the water-supply fountains and so many beautiful buildings. Morosini was a great governor."

"He was nothing but a tyrant," Kostantis scoffed. "On top of that, he surrendered the city to the Turks."

"He did it to save the people, the monuments, and the archives. He had no choice. He was left alone, without any help, nor guns, nor provisions. If he hadn't handed Candia to Köprülü, the Ottomans would've have left no stone standing. They might have killed thousands in their fury after twenty-two years of bloodshed during the siege."

"She's right," Irene said. "That's how Morosini saved the city, and its defenders and their families. Those people had exhausted themselves after decades of fighting."

"Look," sighed Nikolas. "I insist we leave here at once!"

"I'm going out to see the city at any rate," the archaeologist said, stepping out of the courtyard. "If any of you want to, you can come with me."

"We'd better go with her," Irene told the rest of them. "I don't trust her at all. Do you remember last time she left on her own? I can't begin to imagine what she has in mind now. Also, we can't leave her here, can we?"

"Unfortunately, not," Alex said.

"Alright. I'll come with you," Kostantis said, rising.

"What about you, Nikolas?" Irene asked.

"It's against my better judgment, but I'll come. I still think we're making a big mistake. Let's just hope it doesn't turn out too badly."

They said goodbye to the innkeeper, saying they'd be back by nightfall, and left to follow Ariadne. In a short while they were by the port. Opposite them rose the imposing Venetian castle.

"Look!" Ariadne said. "This is the Koules, or, as the Venetians called it, *Roca al Mare* – a rock or fort in the sea. It took them seventeen years to build, from 1523 to 1540…"

"And, as we all know, that's where our adventures started," Kostantis sighed, "from the small room with the sign ENTRY IS STRICTLY FORBIDDEN on the door."

"It feels like centuries since we found the time machine in the Koules," Alex said.

"But it's only been days…" Irene noted.

"And all that because Kostantis tripped and fell on it," Nikolas sneered. "Now here we are, watching the castle in its most glorious era."

"I didn't do it on purpose," Kostantis said. "I'm sorry I've dropped us into this mess."

The archaeologist cut in, "I'm grateful to you, for my part. It's a fabulous experience."

"It'll get even more fabulous if we never return home!"

"No, everything's going to be fine," Irene said, rubbing his back. "We have the machine and we know how it works at last. We'll make it. If not for that earthquake, we'd have been home by now."

"Look at that!" Ariadne gushed. "The port is full of Venetian galleys. How impressive!"

Carried along by her enthusiasm and the majestic spectacle before them, the four friends forgot their fears for a moment and stood admiring the glory of the port of Candia.

"These ships are the descendants of the ancient Athenian trireme," Kostantis said.

They all turned to look at him in astonishment.

"That's right," Ariadne said. "The Venetian galley, an oared vessel, swift and agile, is considered a descendant of the trireme. Look at the *Neorion*, the dockyards. They've pulled some ships in for repairs. The *Neorion* is..."

"Yes, we know what the *Neorion* is," Irene said, rolling her eyes. "Those are the Venetian shipyards and dry docks. There were seventeen of them. Only seven survive in our time."

"It's getting dark. We'd better get moving," Nikolas said. "Mark my words, these strolls can come to no good."

They walked on behind Ariadne until they found the Arsenali Gate to the *Ruga Maistra* – the high street, nowadays one of the most central in Heraklio under the name 25th August – and made their way uphill to the Lions Square.

The light was failing and only a few people milled around. The inhabitants of Candia were turning in early in the years of the siege. They saw many more men than women, and it was difficult to tell the Cretans from the Venetians. The centuries-old Venetian rule had brought the two closers in their daily custom, their culture, even their attire.

There were well-tended buildings on both sides of the street, but some had suffered damage from the Ottoman cannonade. When they arrived before the church of St Titus, Ariadne explained it'd been built by the Byzantine emperor Nicephorus II Phocas. The Venetians refurbished it in the 1500s, and since then it had served as the Catholic cathedral.

"We've travelled to Renaissance Crete with our own guide," Nikolas huffed.

Ariadne was undeterred. "During the Ottoman occupation it was turned into a mosque, the Vizier mosque. It was destroyed in the earthquake of 1856, and rebuilt on the old foundation in 1872. In 1926 it was re-consecrated as a Christian-Orthodox church. The church contained the famous icon of Panaghia Mesopantitissa. Morosini took this icon with him after he surrendered the city. He brought it back to Venice, and in the twenty-first century you can see it there, in the basilica of Santa Maria della Salute."

They ambled towards the *Loggia*. On the roof of the building they saw the Serenissima Republic's flag waving in the breeze.

"This is the *Loggia*, Morosini's headquarters…"

"The fourth *Loggia* the Venetians built, actually," Kostantis said. "The first was built close to the port, the second in 1325 across the square from here." He pointed to the magnificent edifice. "The third Loggia was built at this same spot in 1541, but it was much smaller than this. This one the Venetians built between 1626 and 1628."

They listened attentively, and with a little surprise.

Ariadne took up the thread. "From here the Duke, who's the Governor, or *Provedittore Generale*, presides over military parades and religious processions. From the balconies they read the ducal edicts. If we're lucky, we may see Morosini in person."

"What's this great building across from here?" Nikolas said.

"It's the Duke's Palace," Kostantis said. "It has some fifty rooms, enclosed courtyards, water wells, shops, tanks and cisterns, stables, a club and a prison."

Nikolas thought of their last adventure. "Let's hope we don't end up there," he said.

"This is where Morosini lives, with the members of his council, the *Signoria* as the Venetians called them," Ariadne added.

"Why don't we have that building in our time?"

"The *Palazzo Ducale*, as it was known, will be damaged irreparably during the earthquake of 1810, which destroys almost two-thirds of the city," Kostantis said. "It will be levelled later, in the earthquake of 1856."

As Nikolas lifted his eyes to admire the palace, he noticed an exquisitely beautiful young girl observing them from one of the windows. When she realized he was looking back at her, she disappeared behind thick brocade curtains. He didn't mention it to his friends, but continued to watch the window.

"And this is the renowned St Mark's basilica," Ariadne gushed, bringing Nikolas out of his reverie. "It's the official ducal church of Candia. Tomorrow is the saint's feast day."

"Is it true this is also the dukes' cemetery?" Alex said.

"This is their church. Those who die on the island are buried here,"

"If I remember correctly," Kostantis added, "St Mark's was built in 1239 or thereabouts."

"Yes, but this isn't the original building. That was destroyed in the earthquake of 1303, and then restored by the Venetians. It was restored again after the earthquake of 1508. Following the city's surrender, Köprülü will allot it to his financial advisor, Defterdar, and the church will be called the Defterdar mosque from that time. The worst thing is that the Ottomans will destroy all the great frescoed icons inside. Let's go in and see them."

Without waiting for an answer, Ariadne began climbing the church steps. The four friends followed, looking in awe at the colourful frescoes, the marble sculptures and statues, and the heavy screens, many of which had been given by the dukes.

Ariadne was melancholic. "Look," she said. "The statues you see are the masterpieces of Veneto-Cretan sculpture. See the frescoes? They depict the life of Christ, and the path to human redemption. Look carefully. Nothing of them will survive. We're so fortunate to be able to see them."

Full of emotion, they bowed and made the sign of the cross in front of the icon of the Virgin Mary, praying for a swift return home. Outside, their eyes brimming with tears, they walked slowly to the Morosini fountain, where they drank water and washed their faces. They looked in awe at the statue of Poseidon, imperiously standing at the centre.

As Ariadne told them, Morosini built the fountain as a freshwater reservoir for the city, which until then had suffered from drought. He constructed an aqueduct to transfer water from the slopes of Mount Youchtas to the parched city of Chandax. The fountain had enough outlets for forty people to draw water at the same time. There were bas-reliefs of scenes from Greek mythology and the sea, alongside the coats of arms of the Doge, of Morosini, and of the *Signoria*. It was inaugurated on 25 April, 1628, the feast day of St Mark, the city's patron saint.

Another name for it was the *Gigante* fountain, or the Giant's fountain, because of the great marble statue of Poseidon. In 1847 the Turks added marble columns and the inscription "Abdul Madjid Fountain" in gold-plated script, but in 1900 the monument was restored to its original form.

Kostantis suggested there was a second great fountain in the city.

"Which one would that be?" Nikolas said.

"It's the one at Kornaros Square. Venetians called it the Membo fountain. It was built by Matteo Membo, *Proveditore Generale* of Candia."

"How do you know?"

"It was the first to bring running water to the city. It's decorated with Venetian coats of arms, and a Roman statue."

They had reached Cereals Square, their familiar Lions Square. They watched enchanted as this city reminded them, ever so faintly, of their own. It was almost dark and the wind had picked up. Almost no one walked the streets.

"We must return," Nikolas said, as they heard a terrible roar.

"What was that?"

"Turkish cannon," Ariadne said gravely. "Against the city walls. Some of them must have broken the ceasefire. Nikolas is right. We must go back."

Their heads low, without a word, they walked briskly towards the port. They knew that in a few years the city would be destroyed and its people forced from their homes forever.

They arrived at the inn with sadness in their hearts. As soon as Manousos saw them, he ran out to welcome them back.

"I hope you've enjoyed our city," he said, "even though nowadays it hasn't the glamour it once had. You should've visited before the siege." Then, looking more closely at their dispirited faces, he said, "Is anything the matter, noble lords and ladies?"

"No, thank you, we're just tired," Ariadne said.

"I've prepared two rooms, one for the ladies and one for the masters."

"We may not need them," Irene whispered to her friends. "We must try to set up the machine immediately. With a little luck we'll be back home tonight."

Arete brought a large tray of water, malvasia wine, barley rusks, olives, a skim-milk cheese called *myzethra*, and sweet-smelling warm bread.

"Come, sit down," Manousos said. "The bread is fresh from the oven. Arete is a worthy daughter, is she not? She wants to be a music teacher like her mother, God bless her soul. Have I told you she plays the lute beautifully?"

"How did your wife die?" Ariadne said.

"She was killed by a Turkish round."

"I'm so sorry to hear that."

"God bless you, noble lady," he said.

Arete placed her tray on the table and turned to leave, but her father's voice stopped her. "Arete," he said, "if our guests wish it, you may join them at the great feast tomorrow."

"It would be my pleasure."

"We certainly want to see the great feast," Ariadne said.

They sat around the table and began to eat. From their seats they could see the street, now empty of people except, from time to time, soldiers on patrol.

"Did you have to lie to them?" Irene hissed to Ariadne. "They are such kind people."

"I don't want them to suspect anything's amiss," she said, smiling meaningfully.

Nikolas turned to Alex. "Where have you put the time machine?"

"Here," Alex said, touching the rucksack by his feet.

"Good. As soon as we've eaten, we'll go upstairs to our rooms and get it going – properly for once." Then, turning to Kostantis, he added, "I hope you're feeling steadier on your feet this time!"

"I'm tired of your accusations, you hear? You sound as if I wanted to send us here!" Kostantis said, throwing a hunk of bread at his plate and leaving the table.

As the darkness grew deep and the wind strong, he walked without any idea of where he was going. Irene ran after him. Alex and Nikolas followed.

CHAPTER 3

Irene caught up with Kostantis outside St Peter's church.

"Please, stop!" she called to him. "We have to talk."

"What do we have to say? Nikolas is right. It was my fault. I've brought all that trouble upon you. I wish we'd never found this stupid time machine!"

"You're not responsible, Kostantis. Who could've said what was going to happen?"

"No, it was my carelessness that set the machine going. Now we're wandering across the centuries, not knowing what's around the corner. We don't even know if we're ever going to see our own time again. I want to go home!"

She stepped closer and gently put her arms around his shoulders. "I'm sure in the end we'll return to our families," she said. "Now we know how the machine works – and it was you who found out how. If it weren't for the earthquake, we'd have made it now. You're the ablest one of us all."

"You're just saying that to cheer me up," Kostantis said, wiping the tears from his eyes.

"We've seen and learned so much time-travelling I think it was worth the effort. Imagine our classmates back home – they'd love to be in our shoes."

Her words were soothing to him, and he began to smile again.

Alex and Nikolas arrived panting. "Is he all right?" they said.

"He's fine, but we're all upset. Look what's going on around us."

"Oh, no!" Alex cried.

"What's up now?"

"I left my rucksack back at the inn. With Ariadne!"

"You left her alone with the time machine?" Nikolas cried.

They started running again, towards the inn. Nikolas arrived first and entered, gasping for breath. The room was totally empty. Both Ariadne and the rucksack were gone.

"We've been duped again!" he said. "I told you, we had to leave as soon as possible, but you wanted to take the tour of Venetian Heraklion!"

"I was wrong and I'm sorry," Alex said. "But what are we going to do now?"

Nikolas clicked his finger. "We'll do as we did at Minoan Crete," he said. "We must search for Ariadne and the time machine. Although it may prove more difficult this time round. There isn't anyone to help us."

Kostantis looked fretful. "Do you think she's going to leave us stranded here?"

"I suspect she's going to do something even worse," Irene said.

"Meaning?"

"At Minoan Crete she took the machine to King Minos. I bet now she's going to Morosini."

"Why would she do that?"

"For the same reasons she did then. She'll try to change the flow of history. We must find her as soon as possible. Our only saving grace in this mess is that she doesn't know how the time machine works."

"Neither do we," Nikolas said. "In the previous trip we had Radamanthys, remember? Who's going to help us here?"

There was a knock at the door and Arete walked into the room. "It's late," she told them. "I must go to bed now. When you're finished, I'll show you to your rooms."

"There's our help," Kostantis whispered.

"Are you sure about that?" Nikolas said.

"I believe she's on the level. We'd better let Irene do the talking. She'll trust her."

"Irene, can you make Arete take our side?" Alex said.

"At best she'll think we're mad," Irene said. She stood and walked hesitantly to the girl, who was cleaning somewhere at the back of the restaurant.

"Arete, there's something I want to tell you."

The girl raised her eyes and looked at her nervously, laying aside her cloth. "Whatever you wish, noble maiden."

"We need your help. Please sit with us."

At their table, Arete was bewildered by the glum looks of the young people around her. She fetched a chair and sat next to Irene.

"Is your father asleep?" Nikolas asked.

"Yes."

"Now listen to me carefully," Irene began. "We do not belong in this age. We haven't come from Venice on a ship."

"I thought there was something special about you, noble maiden…"

"We aren't nobility, Arete," Alex said. "We're plain young people like you. We have come from the future. We have a time machine, and we use it to travel. We were in Minoan Crete, and while we were trying to set the machine to take us home, we ended up here by mistake. I know it's difficult to believe, but I swear we're telling you the truth. "

As long as Alex talked, Arete listened avidly. When he finished he looked steadily into her eyes, and she searched their anxious faces one by one without a word. Somehow, she knew they were telling the truth.

"I believe you," she said at last. "I'm not sure how this is happening to you, but I do believe you."

The friends looked at each other gratefully. They had found a new friend and ally.

"Are you going to help us?"

"What could I possibly do for you?"

"You remember the woman who was with us, don't you?"

"Yes, the noblewoman called Ariadne."

"She isn't noble!" Nikolas scoffed. "She's just a thief."

"She took away our time machine," Irene said. "Without the machine we can't go back to our families."

"In what century do you live?"

"About three hundred and fifty years in the future," Alex said.

"How is the world in your time? Us Cretans – do we still exist?"

"We certainly do," Irene smiled. "We are Cretans too. We live in Candia, only in our time it's called Heraklio. Would you like to see the city?"

"How can I see it?"

Alex nudged Nikolas, who took his laptop from his rucksack and turned it on. Strange images formed in front of Arete's widening eyes.

"What kind of magic is this?" she gasped when she saw the photographs.

"This is called technology," Nikolas smiled at her.

Her new friends explained everything she saw – a future of cars, planes, electric light and strange music. She watched speechless, too stunned by what she was seeing to speak.

At last she said, "Do girls learn reading and writing in your age?"

"Boys and girls all go to school – it's the law," Irene smiled.

"If I lived there, could I become a music teacher?"

"You can be anything as long as you study."

"It's my dream to be a music teacher, but my father's poor and Candia's besieged," she said, suddenly saddened.

Kostantis looked at the others for signs of agreement, then offered, "If you want to, and if we can manage to return home, we can take you with us."

For a moment her face lit with happiness. Then she said, "I'd like to very much, but I can't leave my father. But then, since you come from the future, you must know how this siege will end." They could read anguish in her eyes.

No one spoke. They didn't have the heart to tell her that in a few years Candia would fall into Turkish hands.

But they didn't need to speak. Seeing their faces, she realized her city was doomed. All her life she'd longed to see her entire island free. She had no use for dark tidings.

To save them from any awkwardness, she said, "Enough talk. Time for bed. We'll look for your time machine tomorrow. Now come, I have to show you your rooms."

They followed her, guided by her oil lamp. Irene entered a room with Arete while the boys bedded down in the next one. As soon as the three of them were tucked in, Kostantis started on a detailed narrative about the history of Candia. His two friends listened with great interest despite their tiredness. They wanted to know as much as possible about this place, and indeed were sorry they hadn't found out about it before.

"In AD 330," Kostantis began, "Crete became part of the Byzantine Empire, or Eastern Roman Empire, as former part of the Roman state. Its capital then was Gortys. From the seventh century onwards, it was subjected to raids by pirates, mostly Arabs, who used the island as a base for inroads and pillage across the Mediterranean.

" By AD 824 the island was occupied by Arabs from Spain, the Andalusian *muladis*, and was designated an emirate under the name 'Icritis'. The Byzantine emperor Nicephorus II Phocas finally drove them away in the year 961, but not before the Arabs gave the city the name Khandax – in their language Rabd al-Khandaq – which means 'Fort of the Moat', owing to the deep moat they'd dug around it. In Ottoman times the city was called Megalo Kastro, or Great Castle. The name Heraklion became official in 1868…"

"I think I read somewhere that the name goes back to Minoan times," Alex said.

"You're right. I'd forgotten that. Strabo the geographer mentions a port of Knossos called Heraklion at the site of the present city. This name derives not from the famous Herakles, or Hercules, of the twelve labours, but from Herakles Idaeus, one of the Kouretes. Mythology says Rhea entrusted him with the newborn Zeus to save the baby from the wrath of his father, Cronus. The Kouretes are actually considered the first true Cretans and—"

"Tell us about the Venetians," Nikolas cut in. "They are our first concern."

"Well, if you must know, the island was sold to the Venetians in 1204, after the first fall of Constantinople."

"Who dared sell our island?" Nikolas said.

"That was Boniface, Marquis of Montferrat, one of the leaders of the Fourth Crusade. He sold Crete to the Doge Enrico Dandolo for a thousand silver marks at Adrianople. The Venetians had serious problems elsewhere and initially neglected Crete. Taking advantage of that, the Genoese pirate and Count of Malta Henrico Pescatore seized the island in 1206."

Nikolas rolled his eyes, as if the explanation was hardly good enough.

" The Venetians took it back in 1210 and established themselves on the island in 1211. The flying lion of Venice would dominate Crete for more than 400 years, until 1669 when they surrendered it to the Turks. In 1830 the Sultan sold the island to Mehmet Ali of Egypt for 21 million piastres. The Egyptians stayed until 1840…"

"If I remember correctly," Alex said, "the Turks only left Crete for good in 1898."

"That's right. And on 30 May 1913, after much struggle and bloodshed, Crete was united with Greece."

Alex looked at him with something approaching pride. "I didn't realize you knew so much about the history of our island," he said.

"Your other skill is bumping into time machines!" Nikolas said.

Kostantis looked at his friend, pretending to be angry.

"Let's sleep now," Alex yawned. "Tomorrow is going to be a difficult day."

In the next room Arete was telling Irene the history of her family, her life in the besieged city, and the grim struggles of Cretans to overthrow Venetian rule.

"From what I've read," Irene said, "revolts against the Venetian conquerors started very early."

"The first one was in 1212, in the second year of Venetian rule."

"How many revolts have there been?"

"I've counted twenty-seven. The largest was in 1363, led by the Kallergis brothers."

"Do you mean the St Titus apostasy?"

"Exactly!" Arete was surprise by her friend's knowledge. "With the help of the Venetian feudal landlords Crete declared independence. The island took the name St Titus Republic. It only lasted for sixteen months, unfortunately. There was also a great revolt earlier on, in 1273..."

"I think I remember. That must have been the Hortatzis revolt."

"A great family. We're related to the Hortatzis," Arete said, yawning.

"We'd better sleep now. We'll have a hard day tomorrow."

"We'd better. Goodnight."

"Goodnight."

They laid awake for a moment, but fatigue soon overcame them, and they slept dreamlessly.

Alex was up and about before sunrise. He dressed and walked downstairs hoping to meet Arete. She came out of the kitchen to meet him.

"Good morning."

"Morning. Do you have any news?" Alex asked.

"A little. Sit down to eat something first, and I'll tell you."

Alex chose a table by the window. From his seat he could see the galleys that filled the Venetian port, the mild weather and calm sea. Sadness and nostalgia filled his heart. It seemed his home was only a few minutes away. Arete laid on the table a ewer of fresh goat's milk and four cups.

"We can talk when your friends are awake," she said, and made again for the kitchen.

The rest of them showed up before long.

"Any news?" Irene said.

"Arete says she's learned something, but she'll talk to us when she can. Sit down and have some milk. It's wonderful!"

They filled their cups and drank, looking at the port through the window, enchanted. Arete was rushing from table to table to serve the morning customers. When she was finished, she brought a chair and sat beside Irene.

"I woke up before dawn," she said, lowering her voice. "I went around town to see if I could get some information. I asked friends and acquaintances. A merchant told me Ariadne went by his store yesterday. She exchanged a golden pendant for a few sets of clothes."

Irene sighed. "That's her. She sold a gold necklace King Minos had given her to buy these clothes,"

"I asked everywhere, but no-one else had seen her. Then I found my father buying supplies for the inn. He told me Ariadne had been seen by the palace. Do you know what she might be doing there?"

Kostantis thumped his fist on the table. "It's the same story again and again! She wants to talk to Morosini about the time machine."

"We must stop her," Irene said.

"How are we going to do that?" Alex said.

Nikolas looked despondent. "It may already be too late," he said.

As they talked, their panic rising, customers turned to stare at them.

"Please keep your voices down!" Arete hissed. "Listen, I know someone who may help us."

"Who?"

"Bianca, Morosini's niece."

Irene looked confused. "Do you know her well?"

"We've been friends since childhood. My mother was born to nobility, and was on very good terms with the Morosinis. When she decided to marry my father, her own family disowned her."

"Why?"

"My father isn't of noble birth. But, even after my mother was kicked out of home, her old friends stood by her. They admired her for following her heart. On the other hand, she was stripped of all her privileges. In the end she lost her life too. She died fighting the Turks." There were tears in her eyes, and Irene clasped her warmly by the hand.

"I miss her so much, but I remember her with love," Arete said quietly. "She had great courage. She taught me to play the lute and to follow my heart. That's what I'm doing now. When my mother was alive, she helped Bianca learn music, and she'd take me to the palazzo with her. Now I don't go to the palace, but Bianca often visits me. She sings and I play the lute. She has a beautiful singing voice, and knows our local songs as well."

"Where can we meet her?" Nikolas said.

"She'll be at the feast. I'll try to talk to her. She's a good girl, and bright too, and I'm sure she'll help us. I still have a few chores left here, but we can leave afterwards."

"I'll do these," said her father's voice. "Arete, you put on your best clothes and guide our noble youths to the feast."

"Thank you, father," she said and ran up the old wooden staircase.

Manousos started clearing the dishes away. The morning customers had left and the inn was empty again as the four friends were sat quietly, waiting for Arete. At last the innkeeper came to their table.

"I hear that the noblewoman Ariadne has presented herself to the Duke," he told them. "How is it you haven't escorted her?"

"It's very difficult to explain," Irene said.

"I'm ready!" they heard Arete shouting from the top of the staircase, saving them once again from an awkward situation.

When they had a better look at her, they were speechless with awe. She wore a long, dark-blue dress with gold and silver threading at the bust. A blue, gold-embroidered shawl was arranged round her shoulders, and a silk, light-blue, gold-fringed kerchief tied over her hair. Short brown curls crowned her forehead.

"You look beautiful," Alex smiled.

"Your dress is exquisite," Irene said. "I've never seen anything so lovely."

Arete blushed. "It belonged to my mother."

"You look so much like her," her father faltered, his eyes misty with tears. "You're a right noble lass!"

"Thank you, father," she said happily and stepped to the front door.

The others followed. They walked up the *Ruga Maistra*, where throngs of people milled noisily, their faces happy because of the two-day truce. A Mass was going to be held first, then the feast, organized by the Duke. Local men and women in traditional costume, knights in impressive uniform, soldiers, and Venetian nobility in rich attire had congregated in St Mark's Square. At last the Duke of the Kingdom of Candia emerged from his palace and headed for the church, followed by his official retinue.

The crowd was so thick that many had to remain in the churchyard, the five friends among them. As long as they waited for Mass to finish, they scoured the faces in the crowd for any sign of the archaeologist, but she wasn't there. After the end of Mass, Morosini walked to the *Loggia*. He emerged on a balcony there and spoke to the gathering.

Nikolas noticed beside Morosini the girl he had seen the previous afternoon at the window of the ducal palace. He saw to his surprise that Arete approached her and talked to her with obvious familiarity.

So, this is Bianca, Morosini's niece, he thought, watching her admiringly.

When the Duke finished his speech, he retired to the *Loggia* with the nobles and his officials while the people stayed in the square. They talked, ate roast lamb and drank the excellent malvasia. Some were dancing to the sounds of lyres and lutes.

Then the knights paraded in front of the crowd, displaying their suits of armour, spears and javelins, shields, and coats of arms. The tournament would start in a few minutes, and the people clapped and cheered for them. The four friends were enthralled as the tales of knights they'd read were coming alive before their eyes.

Around them, the adults mostly talked about the siege. Their city had been beset for too long, and all were apprehensive. Almost every family had lost someone, and buildings suffered considerable damage. Foodstuffs were becoming scarce, and epidemics were threatening their defences. Yet from each mouth they heard the same whispered phrases:

"We'll fight until not one man is left alive on the ramparts."

"We won't let the heathen befoul our churches."

"Candia will never fall to the Turks."

"Then we'll kick out the Venetians too, and breathe at last as free men."

Listening, the four friends felt proud of the patriotism and courage of Cretans. On the other hand, they knew that in a few years the city would fall to the Ottomans. The people would be forced to leave their homes, the churches would be turned into mosques. Yes, Candia would be liberated in the future, but much more Cretan blood would be shed before then. They watched their compatriots as they sang and danced, knowing they could be dead the next year, the next day. They lingered for a while longer, admiring the square, the fountain, the *Loggia* and the knights readying for their joust, until they saw Arete waving them over.

"We'll talk at the inn, when we're alone," she said.

They walked quickly to the port. Outside St Titus's church they heard military voices and the tramp of boots. As they stopped to find out what was happening, the crowd stood aside. They saw Ariadne in the company of three soldiers. They froze in fear, and then, to their horror, she cried out:

"Those are the traitors. Catch them!"

The crowd turned to see, and instinctively made to grab them. The besieged city wouldn't tolerate even the suspicion of treason among its defenders. The five of them tried to run in panic. Nikolas, the swiftest, managed to escape, but Arete, Irene, Alex and Kostantis were quickly arrested and led to the prison on the ground floor of the ducal palace. Nikolas, heart in mouth, ran through narrow backstreets. He hid in a ruined house until dark, when he thought the soldiers couldn't possibly still be looking for him. He knew he had to get away from the city centre and find a place to spend the night, and when it was dark enough, he slid out of his hiding place and walked to the port. As he reached the Sabbionera Bastion, he noticed a derelict building across from the gate. He decided to take cover there. He reached a lee corner, curled up and closed his eyes, exhausted.

A strong wind blew; the night shrouded the city in a dismal veil. Nikolas was afraid like never before in his life, cold and hungry, and for the first time he felt genuinely far away from home. His hunch that this was going to turn out badly had been proved right. They hadn't listened to him! The thought that his friends were in even greater danger than him was terrifying. As he lay there worrying, tiredness finally subdued him, and he fell asleep on the cold ground.

CHAPTER 4

The sun that rose above the wounded city found the children in the dark dungeons of the ducal palace. They had spent the night in a cell, trying to think of a way to escape. But there was no way out. Weary and hopeless, faces etched with fear, they huddled in a damp and dismal corner or the dungeon.

"Where can Nikolas be now?" Alex said, breaking the silence at last.

"I think he managed to escape," Arete said. "I saw him running to the port."

"I hope he's alright."

"He's bright enough, he'll be fine," Kostantis said. "If they haven't caught him by now, he'll make it. He'd better, he's our only hope."

Alex sighed. "It's definitely worse than last time. But worst of all, we've dragged Arete into it."

"It was my decision to help you," the girl said. "I'm only concerned about my father…"

They heard a loud creak. It was the prison's iron door opening, and one of the three soldiers they'd first seen at Idomeneus Fountain appeared. He was a sinewy, fair-haired, blue-eyed young man, followed by a young woman in a long black cape.

The soldier made room for her. "Your Ladyship," he said, "what we're doing is very dangerous. Please be brief."

She took off her cape and they were surprised to recognize Bianca.

"Go, Knight Fabio. I'll call you when I'm finished," she said. The young man bowed and left.

Now alone, she stepped close to Arete and whispered harshly, "Can you tell me how you're associated with these people? They are accused of treason, and these days that means instant sentencing. Tomorrow morning you may find yourselves in front of the hangman. A rumour is spreading that the entire city is full of spies. The wrath of the people has exploded against you. There's nothing my uncle can do."

Arete looked pleadingly at her. "Do you think I would help traitors?"

"Certainly not, but my opinion doesn't count. You know these aren't my decisions to make.

You're in danger, Arete! Please tell me what's going on. Who are these people?"

"If I tell you the truth, you'll think I'm crazy. At the feast yesterday I explained to you that some friends needed your help. You promised you'd do everything in your power. What I need from you now is to trust me and take us out of this place. When we're safe, I'll explain everything."

"It's impossible to set you free. Even if I attempted it, my uncle's suspicions would immediately fall on me because of our friendship. You're asking me to put my life on the line without even giving me the reason!"

"She's right," Irene cut in. "We must tell her the truth. We have no other option."

"I'm waiting for your answer," Bianca said, ignoring Irene. "We don't have the time."

Irene didn't give Arete a chance to speak. She butted in, recounting all of their adventures to Bianca. Before she'd finished, the noble maiden, who'd been listening with great surprise and concern, took a slow step backwards.

"You're mad if you think I'll believe these lies! Arete, how do you allow them to make fun of me like this? Are you forgetting who I am? Fabio, open the door!"

As the heavy door was closing upon her, Irene shouted in desperation:

"Search for our fourth friend before your uncle's soldiers find him. He can prove what we're telling you. He must be hiding somewhere close to the port. Please help us!"

"She's a great friend, but I wasn't expecting her to believe us," Arete said, her head bowed.

"Give her time," Irene soothed. "I'm sure she'll do something to help you. In her eyes I saw her distress and love for you."

Nikolas was woken at first light by the Turkish cannonade. The wind had dropped, a bright sun was rising above the city, and the ground was wet with morning dew. A few moments passed before he knew where he was. His first thoughts were for his friends: where were they? He must find Manousos, explain as much as possible what had happened, and ask for his help. But first, his friends. He listened as cannonballs hammered at the walls. Another bitter morning for Candia. As he emerged from the ruined building, he was surprised to see a Venetian soldier.

"Follow me!" he said to Nikolas, threatening him with his sword.

Unable to resist, Nikolas followed. The soldier helped him mount a chestnut horse, then he lightly spurred his own white stallion, and they started at a canter. The boy realized they were going away from the city.

Where is he taking me? he thought.

They left the Sabbionera behind them, trotted past the Vitturi Bastion, by the Jesus Bastion, and, following the modern Plastera Street, approached the Martinengo Bastion.

They could see the soldiers in the walls, trying to stem the Turkish attacks. His compatriots were fighting tooth and nail to keep them outside Candia, raining down musket rounds and explosives. Trumpets, church bells and fire alarms sounded throughout the city. The people on the battlements and bastions were warring like lions, showing no fear for their lives. As he watched them fighting for the land of their fathers and families, Nikolas felt proud to be a Cretan. He realized how important it was to sacrifice oneself for a higher purpose. His fear abated, and he wished he could be on the walls too, and fight by their sides.

The horse neighed, pulling him from his daydream. The Venetian had pulled at the reins to make it go faster, and soon they were headed for Bethlehem Gate and the Pantocrator Bastion.

Near the Pantocrator Gate, the modern *Chanioporta*, the soldier helped Nikolas dismount. He tied their horses to a tree and ordered the boy to follow him through narrow streets. Nikolas obeyed, more out of curiosity than fear. He knew he wasn't being taken to prison, at least.

They crossed the street known today as Archiepiskopou Makariou and continued to the St Andreas Bastion. Across from the gate there was a garden with three windmills. The Venetian walked to the nearest of these and pushed at the old wooden door, and Nikolas followed. Inside, the young soldier secured the door behind them.

"I found him!" he shouted to the young woman waiting for them, her arms crossed. It was Bianca.

"What took you so long?" she said.

"I had to avoid the main thoroughfares, so we found a circuitous route. It took me some time to find him too," he said. "He was hiding in an abandoned house near the port, and I ran into him as he was coming out. I was lucky to get him before the morning patrol could arrest him. We've left the horses by the Pantocrator Gate and walked – it's safer. There's a battle and the hunt is on for this lad now. As long as you talk, I'll stand guard outside." He bowed and left them alone.

Nikolas watched the girl with obvious surprise. She was even more beautiful close-up, but she was anxious and looking tired, as if she hadn't slept.

"Your friends are in prison and in danger of being executed," she said. "They've made Arete their accomplice, and she's my best friend. They've filled me with lies about travelling back in time with strange machines." Bianca was almost shouting, beside herself with frustration. "You're their only chance. Can you convince me it isn't a pack of tall tales? I doubt it very much."

"I can certainly convince you," Nikolas said, taking the laptop out of his rucksack. "My friends aren't liars!"

He turned it on, and strange images began unfolding in front of her. As she watched he kept a running commentary.

"How can all those things exist? What kind of magic is this?" Bianca said, turning to him with a look of terror.

"This isn't magic. Those are the inventions of the human mind in the centuries after your own age."

When he'd finished, he closed his laptop, looked at her and said, "I've proved to you we come from the future. As my friends must've told you, we arrived here with the help of a machine that allows us to travel in time. We found it in the castle you've built by the port."

"Does it still exist in your time?"

"It does, as do St Mark's, the *Loggia*, the Lions Fountain, and other Venetian buildings."

"It's amazing," the girl said. She still couldn't believe what she'd seen and heard. "But you must know how the siege ended!"

"Candia will be surrendered to the Turks in 1669."

"Never," she said, indignant. "My uncle will never turn the city over to the heathen."

"Unfortunately, that's what's going to happen," Nikolas said. "Two events guarantee it. The first is treason by the engineer Andrea Barozzi—"

"I know that man!"

"In 1667 he is going to change sides, handing Ahmed Köprülü the city's fortification plans. That's how the Turks will find the weak points in the defences."

"And this is enough to bend the will of my uncle and the defenders of Candia, who have been fighting for so many years?"

"I told you there was a second event, and it's even more significant. In 1669 – in July, if I remember right – the French ship La Thérèse was sunk. The French, who had already lost the Duke of Beaufort in battle, will abandon you. Your uncle will be left alone and helpless, and will be forced to surrender the city to Köprülü on 16th September 1669."

As Nikolas recounted the details of the city's surrender, he silently thanked Kostantis. On the previous night, at Manousos' inn, his friend had told them about the history of their long-suffering birthplace. Now these facts helped him persuade Bianca, and he realized at that moment that a person's real and greatest power is knowledge.

"But what's going to become of us?" Bianca said.

"You'll give up your weapons, and the Turks will let you leave in peace."

"Köprülü will let us leave here alive? I can't believe it!"

"After twenty-two years of siege, and so many casualties to the Turks, Grand Vizier Köprülü will want to end the siege as soon as he can. He's going to accept almost all terms proposed by your uncle," Nikolas tried to calm her. "He's afraid, of course, of the Sultan's wrath. That's Mehmed IV."

"If we know what's going to happen, we have to warn my uncle. We can save Candia!"

"Don't even think about it! Any intervention in history may change things for the worse."

"Don't you want the deliverance of Candia?"

Nikolas realized it was a mistake to reveal the future to her. She'd do anything to save her city. "And do you think your uncle will believe you?" he said.

"You're going to convince him!"

"We don't have the right to change the future. Even if we try, we can't be sure the city will be saved. We may cause greater damage. Maybe more lives will be lost. A people must learn from their history, and so history must remain undisturbed. What I can tell you for sure is that in the end Candia will be returned to the people it really belongs to. And, what's more, the people of letters who leave here will enlighten the whole of Europe with their intellect."

Bianca looked confused, trying to understand what he meant. She didn't speak for a while, then her fingers found the golden cross around her neck.

"Yes, it isn't right to change what God has preordained for us," she sighed.

Nikolas looked at her relieved. "Now that you know the truth, will you help me free my friends?"

"It's difficult to get them out of prison, but not impossible. Tell me about that strange woman my uncle received at the palace, the one who accused you of treason."

"We came together from the future. She was the one who stole our time machine. Without it we can't return to our time or see our families again."

"I know how that feels," Bianca said sadly. "Many people I know have been killed in the siege, and I can't say whether I may meet my friends and family again."

"So, you understand how I feel. Please help us," he begged.

She raised her head in resolution. "I must first think of a way to liberate your friends from prison," she said. "Afterwards we must find that woman. I'll do everything possible. You must wait for me here. Stay hidden!"

"Thank you. Whatever happens, I know you'll try your best."

Bianca looked tenderly at Nikolas, opened the rickety door and left the ancient windmill in the company of Fabio.

The rain had started afresh and a strong north wind had risen. It swept the rain upon tiled roofs and howled eerily in the alleyways. It was the 26th of April in the year 1665. Candia was ever more hard-pressed by Turkish attacks.

A considerable part of the city was in ruins. Many houses had been damaged by Turkish artillery. Foodstuffs were scarce and epidemics were a constant threat.

Even after eighteen years of fruitless siege, the Sultan wouldn't retreat. Cretan people resisted heroically, and Morosini wasn't inclined to surrender. Bianca knew how this was going to end, but had no means of changing it. These were the dark thoughts that occupied her.

She looked through the window of her room to the torches flickering on the battlements, otherworldly through the raindrops dancing in the wind.

She had asked to be received by her uncle and now waited for his summons. She was turning over in her mind what she was could say that would save Arete and the other children.

Her thoughts were cut short by loud voices and clangs. She stepped into the corridor, to find the source of the noise. There she ran into Fabio, who was coming to meet her.

"The decision has been made," he said. "They'll be executed tomorrow morning. You'd better stay in your room."

Pushing past him, Bianca ran to the Council chamber.

"I must speak to my uncle at once!" she told the guards outside.

"I'm sorry, Lady, but a council of war is in process, and I have orders not to let anyone disturb the Governor, for any reason at all."

"It's a matter of life or death!" she cried.

"I'm sorry, Lady," the officer repeated and stood resolutely before the door.

She lowered her eyes and returned to her room. Fabio tried in vain to soothe her.

"We must do something! They're going to hang them at dawn," she said through her tears. "Please, find a way to help them!"

The young man thought for a while, then looked at her, and said firmly, "I have an idea. You must go to the old windmill to find Nikolas as soon as it's light. You'll stay there and wait for me."

"What are you proposing?"

"I'll try to free them for your sake."

"Be careful!" she gasped.

"I'd give my life for you, Lady Bianca," he said, and left before she could utter another word.

CHAPTER 5

At dawn, Alex, Kostantis, Irene and Arete were walking soundlessly behind the soldiers who would lead them to the gallows.

When the prison officer had announced Morosini's decree, they'd tried in vain to convince him of their innocence with cries and tears. They asked to speak to the Duke, but no-one would listen to them. Now they walked, heads bent, towards the scaffold set on the *Piazza delle Biade*, the Cereals Square, near the great plane tree. The rain had stopped, but the sky was filled with dark clouds pregnant with rain.

Ariadne was among the crowd that thronged the square. Looking at them she realized the disaster her lies had caused. It wasn't her intention to destroy the four friends, she had only wanted to remove them from her plans. The Duke had summarily decided to execute them, but only to pacify his people, seething with rage at the traitors walking among them.

They, on the other hand, couldn't explain how they had entered Candia. Ariadne's idea was to have the children arrested by Morosini, so she could steal their laptop. That was the only way she could persuade him she was a time traveller. If she could achieve this, she might change history and save Crete. But Morosini had kicked her out of the *palazzo*, in the belief she was deranged.

Looking at the four youngsters, she tried to think of a way to help them. But it was too late. They were walking to the scaffold through the jeering voices of a crowd mad with revenge. Not being able to stand her remorse, she decided to act. She took the time machine out of her satchel and ran into the crowd, trying to reach the scaffold. If her plan worked, she might be able to save the children there and then.

Then a booming sound was heard and the square filled with smoke. Panic followed as townspeople ran for cover from the Turkish cannon, and from the heavy rain that fell.

The archaeologist was trying to make out the faces of the children among the crowd. She knew they had vanished from the scaffold, and she immediately realized that someone had helped them escape. The explosion was therefore an act of diversion, not a Turkish attack. The rain! It was blind luck! A smile of relief formed on her lips.

She tried to run against the throng sweeping her towards the *Voltone* Gate, along the modern Kalokairinou Street – or *Strada Larga*, as it was called by the Venetians. As soon as she managed to free herself the crowd, she made for the backstreets to search for Irene, Alex and Kostantis, hoping against hope to find them there. As she was reaching the *Chanioporta*, she heard heavy footsteps behind her. She turned around, but before she had any time to react, a tall Venetian knight was showing her the tip of his sword.

"Follow me!" he grunted.

She complied without a second's thought, and he led her through cobbled alleys to the *San Andrea* Bastion. With the tip of his sword at her back, he made her walk towards the three windmills, and ordered her to stop at the nearest. He opened the wooden door and pushed her inside.

"Well done!" Bianca told Fabio when she saw him.

"It wasn't difficult," he said, looking menacingly at Ariadne.

"So, here you are," Ariadne said, shaking her head. "I knew you were up to something."

"Cut the crap and give us back the time machine," Irene said, mad with anger.

"We almost died because of you," Nikolas added.

Fabio stepped close to Ariadne, snatched her rucksack and handed it to Bianca. She passed it on to Nikolas.

"Thank you. We owe you our lives," he said, his voice trembling. "You are real gentlefolk!"

"You owe everything to Fabio," she answered, looking gratefully at the young knight, her heart gladdening. "Tell me now, how did you manage this?" she asked.

"Two of my companions helped me. They're my friends. We know each other from Venice."

"Yes, but how?"

"I planned everything with their help," he said. "Last night we hid a powder keg near the Cereals Warehouse. When the youngsters stepped on the scaffold just now, Angelo set fire to it."

"Weren't people endangered by the explosion?"

"My friends are well versed in the arts of war," he said, looking wounded.

"I don't question your abilities," Bianca said gently. "Not for a moment."

He gave her a tender look. "Vincenzo stood by the scaffold," he said. "As soon as the powder went off he took advantage of the panic and the rain to hide the youngsters in a cart. Under cover of the smoke he drove here. I had already recognized this woman in the crowd. I followed her, arrested her and brought her to you."

"Thank you for everything," Bianca said, deeply moved. "You're a true knight."

Fabio bowed. "I promised I'd do anything for you. More than that, we can't let innocent people die. And friends of yours can't possibly be traitors."

The four friends thanked him, Arete and Bianca.

"Now fix your machine and get going!" Bianca told them. "You don't have much time left. This isn't a big city. Someone may have seen us. We may be arrested, and this time there'd be nothing I could do."

Kostantis, Nikolas and Alex stood over the time machine, trying to tune it to home. Ariadne pushed to get near them.

"Stay away if you want to come with us!" Nikolas said. "We could happily leave you here."

"You don't understand how deeply you have involved our friends in this," she said, narrowing her eyes. "Morosini must have been told of your escape. His suspicions will immediately fall on his niece because of her friendship with Arete. If you leave them here, they face almost certain death. He'll believe they've aided the city's traitors."

"You did your best to convince him!" Nikolas shouted.

"I was only able to persuade him on this, regrettably."

"How did you do it?"

"Don't forget I know the history of Candia. It wasn't too difficult. The Vizier's spies are everywhere. You helped too. You couldn't explain who you are and how you arrived at Candia."

They realized she had a point: Arete, Bianca and Fabio were in mortal danger – not to forget Angelo and Vincenzo.

"You go now. Don't worry about us," Fabio said, discerning the anguish in their eyes.

"But we can't leave you to your fate now, we just can't," Alex said. "You've saved our lives!"

"We'll pull through," Arete said.

"Enough talk! We aren't going without you," Kostantis said, making the final adjustments to the time-machine.

"I can't come with you," Arete said. "I'm not leaving my father, or Candia."

"I can't come either," Bianca said. "This is my second home."

"Then we aren't going," Irene cried. "We can't leave so many people in danger because of us."

"Stop talking nonsense," Arete jested. "We'll find a way to prove to the Duke we haven't aided any spies."

The archaeologist's lips drew into a smile. She had predicted the generosity of those children, and knew they wouldn't abandon their friends as long as they were in danger. This would give her time to make new plans.

"The time machine is ready," Kostantis said. "No more talk. Come with us!"

His words were cut short by the harsh sound of the door of the old windmill as it crashed open. A Venetian official strode in, escorted by four soldiers.

The friends panicked when they saw him. Kostantis thought for a moment to push the Start button and make them disappear, but immediately decided against it. The time-eddy could probably suck all of them inside.

The noble stepped towards Bianca. "I demand an explanation!" he said.

"Sir Pietro, please let them go," she said softly.

"No-one's going anywhere. Tell me at once what's been going on. These persons have been condemned to death for treason, but you liberated them against the orders of the *Signoria*."

"These kids aren't traitors, they haven't hurt anyone," Bianca said. "It's just that they found themselves in the wrong age."

"What did you say?" the official said, alarm forming behind his eyes. It was then he saw the time machine. He stepped towards it as if entranced.

"This can't be possible," he said. "Who are you?"

"I can explain," Bianca said.

She'd known this man for a long time. He was her uncle's right-hand man and most trusted friend. Pietro Longobardo was his name, a nobleman with roots in Lombardy, but everyone knew he'd been born and raised in Verona. He had studied medicine and philosophy at the University of Padua, and was one of the most famous medical doctors and philosophers of his time. The Doge Domenico II Contarini, having recognized his ability, invited him to Venice as an advisor. When Morosini was appointed Duke to the Kingdom of Candia, Pietro asked Contarini to be granted office in Morosini's court. The Doge allowed him to follow Morosini to Candia, but never understood why Longobardo left a splendid career in Venice to live on that island.

Bianca had known him since she was a toddler, a man buried in his books, studying medicine, philosophy, poetry, music. He was the one who introduced her to Vasiliki, Arete's mother, who became her music teacher. He always treated her like a father.

Bianca stood by him. "I'll tell you a story that'll sound impossible to you, but you know I never lie."

Pietro ignored her. All his attention was on the machine.

"This is a time machine," he said, and took it in his hands.

The four friends looked at each other, and then at him, in shock. Alex wondered for a moment if Alex's grandfather had passed through here too, if he had met Pietro Longobardo, as he had met

Zakros in Minoan Crete. Fabio, Bianca and Arete couldn't make sense of it.

Alex turned to the man. "This time machine belonged to my grandfather," he said. "Perhaps you met him? Do you know where he is? My mother has been looking for him for many years."

Pietro stared back at the boy. Tears clouded his eyes and streamed to his beard. He managed to sit on a millstone, still holding the machine.

"I was certain my grandson would follow in my tracks. I made sure, by leaving the map for you to find. I'm proud of you and your friends," he said, looking closely at the boy.

"How do you mean?" Alex said.

"My real name isn't Pietro, it's Alexandros, Alex, the same as yours."

The boy looked closely at the Venetian and saw there, just for a moment, saw something familiar in his face.

"Granddad!"

"Yes, my boy. It's me," the old man said and took Alex in his arms.

As they wept and hugged, the others looked on, puzzled and moved. It was a long time before anyone could utter a word.

"Grandfather, what happened?" Alex said. "Why didn't you come home?"

"I'll explain everything in good time. But tell me first, how did you find the time machine?"

Alex took up the tale, told him how and where they found it, their trip to Minoan Crete, and their meeting with Zakros.

"So, you've met my friend Zakros!" his grandfather laughed.

"He actually persuaded Minos to let us leave there," Alex said.

"Then how did you travel here?"

"It was a mistake. When we'd set up the machine to leave, there was a great earthquake, and I think the chronometer went out of alignment."

"I know, I know. It's too sensitive, needs a lot of attention."

"Why are you here? Why didn't you return? Mother is still looking for you."

"Candia needed me more. I haven't had the heart to leave this city. The people here need my knowledge and my help. It isn't by chance that this siege has lasted for so many years."

"Was there ever a Pietro Longobardo?" Bianca said.

"No, my dear girl," he said, smoothing her hair. "Many years ago, when I was a young archaeologist, I discovered the machine on a dig in Mexico. To be exact, it was given to me by Yoom, the queen of the Guhula tribe. It took me years to understand how it worked. When I started to operate it, I began travelling back in time."

"Why did you go back?" Kostantis said. "I'd have travelled to the future."

"I was an archaeologist. I wanted to see with my own eyes what I'd been studying for so many years. It's an experience I still can't put into words."

"We know it," Nikolas said.

The old man turned to look at the boy, who was nodding smugly.

"Tell us, Sir Pietro, what happened?" Bianca said, moving to sit beside him.

"During one of my journeys I came to Venice and decided to settle there for some time," he said. "I was always fascinated by the Renaissance. I created an alias, Pietro Longobardo, so that I might move freely. My knowledge soon made me rather famous, and my services were in demand. The Doge offered me a post as his doctor and adviser. By that time, I'd met Morosini and become his friend. When the Doge appointed Morosini Duke to the Kingdom of Candia, I asked to be posted there with him. He refused at first, but after I pressed him, he allowed me to come to my beloved island."

"And then?" Irene said.

"Then the siege began, and my only care was how to help my compatriots defend Candia against the Turks…"

"So, it's because of you that Candia has lasted for so long!" Alex said.

"The bravery, self-sacrifice and love for the homeland Cretans have shown kept the Turks outside the walls for twenty-two years. I may have played a small part in that," he said with a thin smile.

"Why did you hide the machine at the Koules?"

"I did it because I knew the Koules would survive in time. I hoped my only grandson might find it someday. He's always been curious and clever. I just didn't realize how clever, or that he'd find the machine so soon."

At that moment they heard a terrible sound and ran to the door.

"What was that?" Kostantis said. "It sounded too close."

"Turkish artillery," Pietro said calmly. "Make ready to leave."

"Aren't you coming with us?" Alex said. "Mother would love to see you!"

"And I'd love to hold her in my arms, but I can't, young man. I must stay here to the end. Please kiss her for me, and tell her that duty prevails upon me to stay. I'll be back to take you along. I want you to promise that as soon as you go back, you'll hide the time machine in a safe place. You are never to use it again. Your lives are in danger!"

"I promise," Alex said.

"When the time comes, you'll learn everything you need to know. For now, you're still young, but on your twenty-fifth birthday you'll go back to the Koules, and there you'll find the answers to all your questions. But I want you to promise me you'll never use the machine in the future," he said firmly. "I'll tell you everything one day, but that day hasn't come yet."

His grandfather's face seemed to forbid questions, yet Alex said, "I'd like to ask a favour of you before we leave."

"You may ask me anything."

"Please help Arete travel to Venice. She wants to be a music teacher, like her mother."

Pietro looked at the girl and answered with a smile, "She's going to be a famous musician."

"Bianca, Arete, please take care of my granddad!"

"We will," they said in unison. "We may never see you again," Bianca added, trying to hide the tears behind a white lace kerchief. "But we will remember you every day." Arete clasped her friend's hand.

They thanked Bianca, Arete, Fabio and Pietro, falling warmly into one another's arms, knowing they'd probably never meet again. Then they made ready to jump once again though time.

Alex wrapped his arms around his grandfather. At least now he knew now why his family had missed him for so long.

"You're wrong to leave the time machine in the hands of ignorant children!" Ariadne hissed at

Pietro. It was unusual for her to have stayed silent for so long.

"Who are you?" the old man asked.

"My name is Ariadne, and I'm an archaeologist, like you." The old man was startled at the sound of her name. She looked at him in surprise.

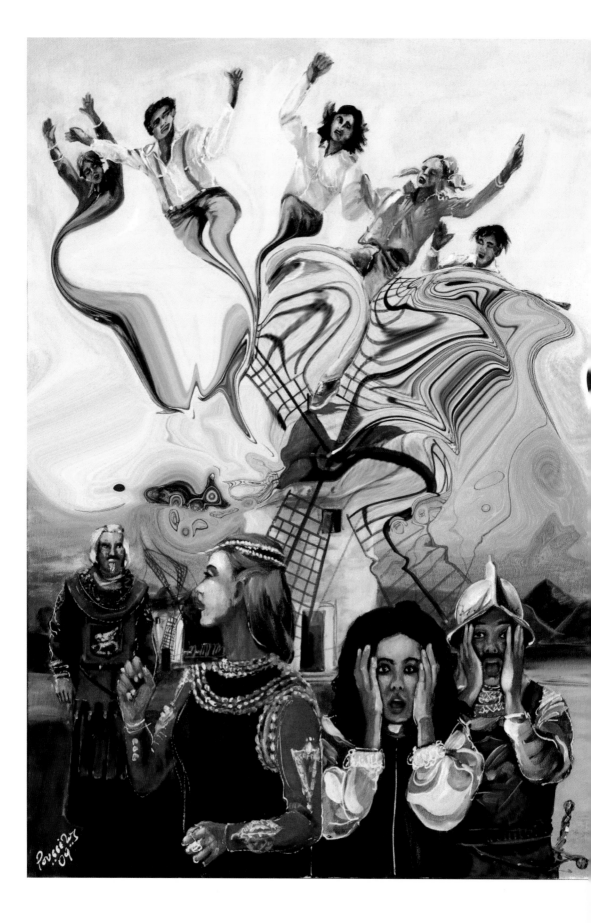

"She's following us, she tries to steal the time machine," Nikolas snapped. "She was the one who denounced us. We almost died because of her."

"Why don't you use the machine and your knowledge to save Candia?" Ariadne demanded. "This device and the information we have, imagine what we could do together. Change the future! Save Candia! Change the entire world!"

"Don't listen to her, grandfather!" Irene said. "You know it's not right to interfere in situations above our decree."

Pietro looked curiously at Ariadne. "Candia will be surrendered, but, as you know, it won't be lost," he said finally, bitterly. "It will be returned to the people it belongs to in the future. It seems God has decided that Cretans must shed even more blood. He must have a reason. What we have to do is fight to the end."

"I want to stay here," Ariadne said.

"Good, we'll get rid of her at last," Irene said. "Thank you, grandfather Alexandros!"

"You can't stay," Pietro said. "Your destiny lies elsewhere."

"I don't understand you."

"You'll understand in time," the old man said. He stepped to Kostantis and handed him the time machine.

The travellers huddled around their machine. With quick hands, the boy started to set the chronometer.

"Come on, Kostantis. Are you ever going to push Start?" Nikolas shouted.

"I've already pushed it," Kostantis said.

"Then why doesn't it work?"

"I've no idea."

"Let me have a look," Pietro said.

As he approached, a great boom was heard and the old mill began falling down around them, as if a tunnel filled with gunpowder had detonated under their feet. Kostantis fell upon the time machine, which emitted a blinding flash that shrouded them in whiteness. The earth under their feet was shaking from the explosion. They felt an intense giddiness, but before they lost their senses altogether, Pietro Longobardo, Bianca, Arete and Fabio had time to watch an eddy of light swirling the four friends and the archaeologist again in time.

Arete was sitting by the window. The storm had abated and the heavy clouds cleared. She was looking at a sea coloured by the westering sun.

She took the lute in her hands and began to play a melancholy tune.

"Are you well, my child?" Manousos asked.

"I'm fine, father. You can rest now. I won't be long."

"You look very sad to me, as if something is weighing upon you."

"There's a weight on all of us, father."

He kissed his daughter's brow and stepped onto the old wooden stairway.

The girl was wondering whether her friends had arrived safely home or were still wandering, lost in time.

She lifted the earthenware lamp, walked to her room with tired steps, and lay on her bed. Her last thought was that Candia was going to be lost in a few short years. Her heart gave an anguished flutter. Tears stained her white lace pillowcase, the last gift she had from her mother.

Myriad crows flew o'er Minos's city,
For war brought fiercest Ottoman hordes.
Long suffered Candia under siege, without pity
—Fairest Cretan town, every book records.
Years two-and-twenty the longest siege lasted,
Köprülü heeded not Venice, lion and valour.
Only betrayal could now best the besieged:
Barozzi thus cast his family's name in dishonour.
Turks at last entered Chandax, in pillage ecstatic,
Left nothing to stand, but tall mosques they erected.
O Candia of song, once you did reign majestic;
Heathen enjoy you now, we listen dejected.
  (If humans' sanctities are befouled, it's sensed,
  Only in blood may the offence be cleansed).

Written by Arete of Candia,
In the month of April, 1674

Printed in Great Britain
by Amazon

78720212R10054